The Chick That Wouldn't Hatch

The Chick That Wouldn't Hatch

Claire Daniel

Illustrated by Lisa Campbell Ernst

Green Light Readers
Harcourt Brace & Company
San Diego   New York   London

First Green Light Readers edition 1999
Green Light Readers is a trademark of Harcourt Brace & Company.

Library of Congress Cataloging-in-Publication Data
Daniel, Claire.
The chick that wouldn't hatch/written by Claire Daniel;
illustrated by Lisa Campbell Ernst.
p. cm.—(Green Light Readers)
Summary: Before she hatches from her egg, a baby chick takes quite a trip around
the farm—with her mother and other animals in pursuit.
ISBN 0-15-202337-2
ISBN 0-15-202269-4 pb
[1. Eggs—Fiction. 2. Chicken—Fiction.] I. Ernst, Lisa Campbell, ill.
II. Title. III. Series.
PZ7.D216Ch 1999
[E]—dc21   98-55235

A C E F D B

There were six eggs in Hen's nest.
Chip! Chip! Out popped five chicks.

"My family!" cried Hen.
One egg didn't hatch. It rolled out of the nest.

"Stop that egg!" Hen called.
The egg kept going.

It rolled over and over, past the pigpen.
"Stop that egg!" Hen called.

Pig couldn't catch it, so he ran, too.
The egg kept going.

It rolled over and over, past the pond.
"Stop that egg!" called Hen and Pig.

Duck couldn't catch it, so she ran, too.
The egg <u>kept</u> going.

keep

It rolled over again and again, past the
tomato patch.
"Stop that egg!" called Hen and Pig and Duck.

Horse couldn't catch it, so he ran, too.
The egg skipped over a ditch.

"Stop! Stop!" cried Hen.
It hopped over a fox.

The egg rolled into the shed and hit the wall. *CRACK!* The chick that wouldn't hatch had hatched!

"My baby!" Hen cried.

"Mom!" said the chick. "What a ride I had!"

"Yes," said Hen, "and what a run we had!"

Display type set in Litterbox
Text set in Minion
Color separations by Bright Arts Ltd., Hong Kong
Printed by South China Printing Company, Ltd., Hong Kong
This book was printed on 140-gsm matte art paper.
Production supervision by Stanley Redfern and Ginger Boyer
Designed by Barry Age